LITTLE
GOOD
WOLF

For all of our Little Grandwolves—
Margot, Ellen, Sophia, Matthew, McKinley,
Addison, Jackson, and Rafe
—Janet and Susan

Clarion Books is an imprint of HarperCollins Publishers.

Little Good Wolf
Text copyright © 2022 by Susan Stevens Crummel
Illustrations copyright © 2022 by Janet Stevens

The Library of Congress Cataloging-in-Publication Data has been applied for.
ISBN: 978-0-35-856188-0

The illustrations in this book were done in mixed media.
The text was set in 1822 Caslon Pro and Koara.
Cover and interior design by Cara Llewellyn.

Manufactured in Italy
RTLO 10 9 8 7 6 5 4 3 2 1
✻
First Edition

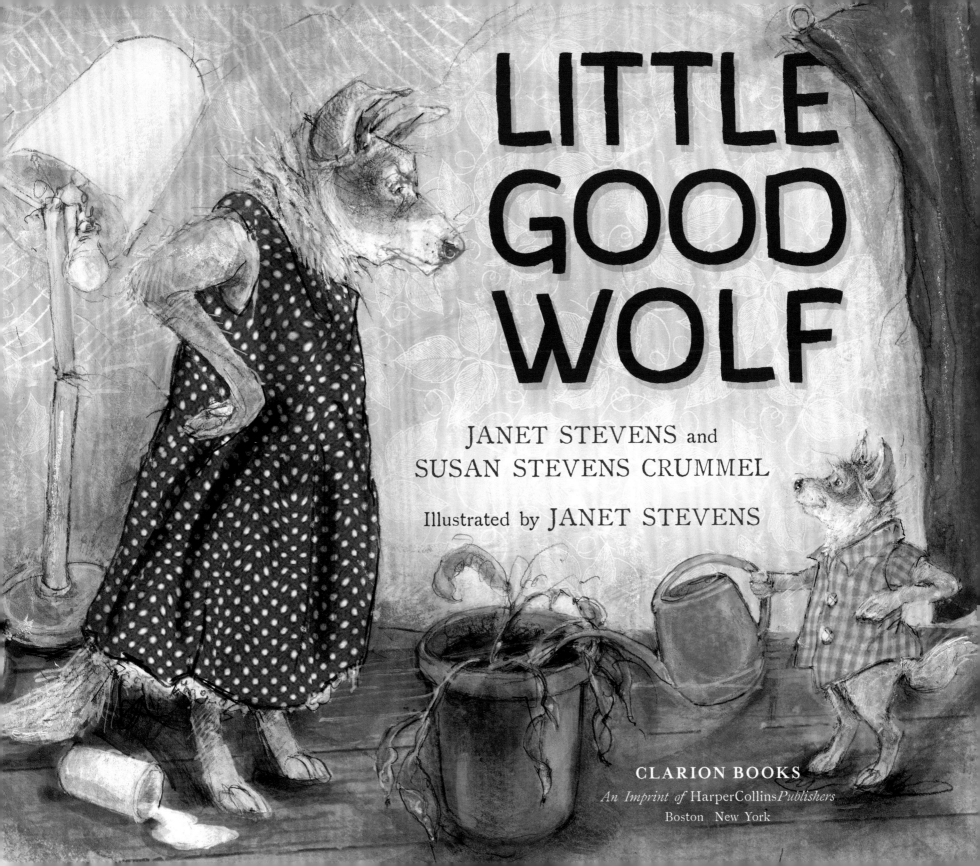

LITTLE
GOOD
WOLF

JANET STEVENS and
SUSAN STEVENS CRUMMEL

Illustrated by JANET STEVENS

CLARION BOOKS
An Imprint of HarperCollinsPublishers
Boston   New York

Once upon a time, deep in the Big Bad Forest,
there lived a family of wolves. But they were not happy.

"Our son is hopeless," groaned Papa Wolf.

"And we've tried everything," moaned Mama Wolf.
"Timeout. Extra chores. No dessert. Nothing works . . ."

". . . He takes baths.

He plays with piggies.

He cleans his room.

He brushes his teeth.

He even reads bedtime stories *by himself!*"

"Impossible!" cried Papa Wolf. "We are
Big Bad Wolves and you are *good*?
A Little *Good* Wolf? You will *never* fill
my big bad shoes!"

"But, Papa, you don't wear shoes,"
replied Little Good Wolf.

"I mean, you'll never be like me!"
yelled Papa Wolf.

"I'm sorry," said Little Good Wolf.

"Big Bad Wolves don't say 'I'm sorry!'"

"I'm sorry I said 'I'm sorry.'"

"Aaaaaahh!" cried Papa Wolf.

"There's no choice." Mama Wolf sighed.
"We must send him to . . ."

So off went Little Good Wolf on the Big Bad Bus to the rottenest, nastiest, most horrible school the world has ever known, the Big Bad School.

"So *you* must be the new student," snorted Prince A. Bull. "You're *late!* Giant is waiting."

LESSON 1
BASIC BADNESS
TEACHER: GIANT

"FEE! FIE! FOE! FOO! I smell *you*! A *good* wolf? EWWWW!"

"Hello, Mr. Giant," said Little Good Wolf. "Wow! What nice big feet you have."

"All the better to stomp you with!" roared Giant.

"Wow! What a nice big club you have, Mr. Giant."

"All the better to whomp you with!"

"Wait, I have an idea!" Little Good Wolf grabbed a ball and tossed it in the air. "Whomp *this* instead of *me!*"

Giant swung.

WHOMP!

Little Good Wolf clapped. "What a hit!
You could play baseball . . . for the Giants!
Wouldn't that be fun?"

"Stop!" cried Prince A. Bull.
"No *fun* allowed at Bad School!
Next lesson."

LESSON 2
BAD ATTITUDE

TEACHER:
WICKED STEPMOTHER
TEACHING ASSISTANTS:
WICKED STEPSISTERS

"Pay attention, Wolf," snapped Wicked Stepmother.
"To be truly bad, you must be rude, selfish,
and a slob. Make messes, then demand
others clean up. Never make your bed.
Never pick up your clothes. Never put your toys—"
"Gimme that dress!" interrupted one Wicked Stepsister.
"It's MY dress, you lost yours," said the other.
"Where's my doll?"
"I can't find anything in this mess."
"It's your fault!"

"Wait, I have an idea!" Little Good Wolf sprang into action. "Hang up dresses. Fold the shirts. Toys on shelves—puzzles here, dolls there. Now you'll know exactly where everything is and what belongs to whom. Doesn't your room look tidy?"

"Stop!" yelled Prince A. Bull.
"No *tidiness* allowed at Bad School!
Next lesson."

"Gobble, gobble, slurp, slurp, slurp. Eat it fast so you can

BUUURRRRP!"

Troll said before shoving a whole slice of pizza into his mouth.

"Excuse me, Mr. Troll. Does your pizza *taste* good?" asked Little Good Wolf.

"I don't know," Troll answered.

"Wait, I have an idea! Take a small bite. Chew it slowly," said Little Good Wolf. "Taste the creamy cheese? The spicy sauce? The crunchy crust? You'll have more food in your tummy and less on your face—which is much more polite!"

"Stop!" screamed Prince A. Bull. "No *politeness* allowed at Bad School! Next lesson."

"Huffing and puffing are essential skills, especially for Big Bad Wolves," instructed Dragon. "Blowing down houses is a must. Fire breathing is for fun, see?"

WHOOSH!

"You really do fire things up!" cried Little Good Wolf. "Wait, I have an idea! Just think, one *whoosh* and you could light a cake full of birthday candles. You'd be the life of the party!"

"Stop!" bellowed Prince A. Bull.

"No *parties* allowed at Bad School!

That's it! You're expelled!"

When the Big Bad Bus came to take him home,
Little Good Wolf was nowhere to be found.

The forest grew deeper and darker as he walked, alone and afraid.
He couldn't go home. But where could he go?

"Having a bad day?" Old Hag appeared
suddenly from the darkness.

"How did you know?" asked Little Good Wolf.

"Bad news travels fast," she replied. "Can I help?"

"It's hopeless," Little Good Wolf said. "No one
likes me the way I am. They want me to change."

"I see. But would you change—if you could?"

Little Good Wolf sighed. "I want Papa and
Mama to love me."

Old Hag held up a glossy red apple.
"One bite and good turns to bad. One bite
and Little Good Wolf becomes Little Bad
Wolf—the apple of his papa's eye."

"But," she warned, "you must be careful.
This apple also works the other way—one bite
and BAD becomes GOOD."

Little Good Wolf didn't know what to do.

"Come, my pretty. Take the apple."

Little Good Wolf held the apple to his mouth.

Old Hag leaned closer
and said, "One BIG BAD BITE."

Suddenly afraid, Little Good Wolf quickly
turned and ran into the forest.

With every step Little Good Wolf thought of
how much he missed his mama and papa.

What he didn't know was that his mama and papa missed him, too. In fact, their big bad hearts were broken.

"Howl,"

Little Good Wolf called back,
following the sound . . .

. . . until he could see the lights of their house
through the trees. "Mama! Papa! I'm home!"

They cried. They hugged.
They jumped for joy.

"We missed you, Little Good Wolf," said Papa Wolf and Mama Wolf. "We missed you *so much* that we actually did some *good* things!"

"You *did?*"

"Yes!" answered Mama Wolf. "I caught a piggy and didn't eat him. I *kissed* him!"

"And I *combed* my *teeth*," added Papa Wolf.

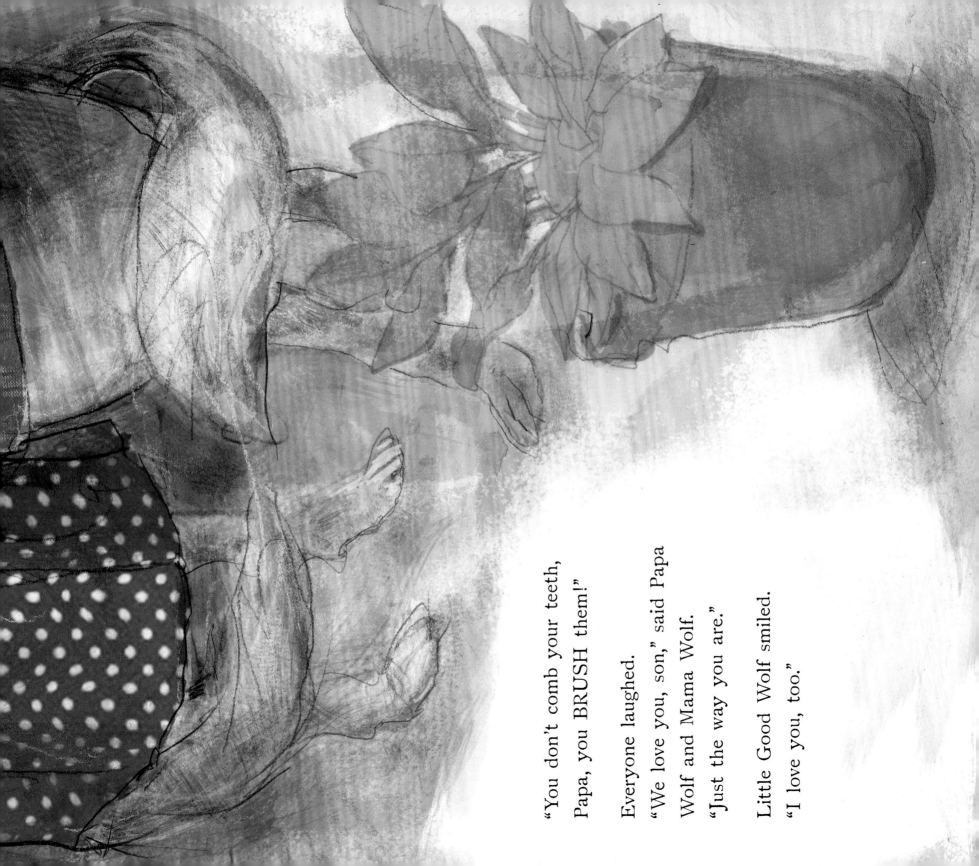

"You don't comb your teeth,
Papa, you BRUSH them!"

Everyone laughed.
"We love you, son," said Papa
Wolf and Mama Wolf.
"Just the way you are."

Little Good Wolf smiled.
"I love you, too."

Deep in the Big Bad Forest, there lived a family of wolves—different, interesting wolves. And they all lived happily ever after.

Or did they?